# HATCHiMALS™
# HATCH FRIENDS FOREVER!

### STICKER ACTIVITY BOOK

## BFF SOS!

Cheetree can't find his best friend, Albasloth. Can you get the Hatchimals back together again? Find Albasloth on your sticker sheet and add him here.

## HATCH...

Albasloth has a blue body, a little pink nose, and silvery wings.

# HATCHTOPIA HANGOUTS!

The clouds have cleared and there are some new locations to spot in Hatchtopia! Can you find the missing places on your sticker sheet, and then fill in the name that goes with each location?

## PLACE NAMES

**PETAL PATH**

**RHYTHM RAINBOW**

**BREEZY BEACH**

**MOONLIGHT MOUNTAIN**

**FRIENDSHIP FARM**

**THE HATCHERY NURSERY**

# SURPRISE!

Don't you love surprises? When you hold a Hatchimal egg in your hand, there's no way to guess who's inside! There are three exciting Hatchimals hiding on this page. Study the clue chains, then stick in the correct pictures and write their names underneath.

**DID YOU KNOW . . . ?**

Surprise Hatchimals come in pairs, so each of these little buddies has a twin!

**1**

Who am I?

▼

My mane is fluffy.

▼

My name begins with the letter L.

▼

I love to roar!

▼

**2**

Who am I?

▼

I am super stripy.

▼

My name begins with the letter Z.

▼

I don't have whiskers.

▼

**3**

Who am I?

▼

I have a heart on my tummy.

▼

My name begins with the letter P.

▼

My ears are floppy.

▼

4

# FARM FUN

These best buddies are on a trip to Friendship Farm. But their picture has been scrambled, and the gang has been split up! Look carefully, then put the picture strips into the right order to bring everyone back together again.

**DID YOU KNOW . . . ?**
There's always something for you and your pals to do at Friendship Farm! All the best hatchy birthday parties happen here.

A   B   C   D   E

Write the correct sequence here.

Finished? Now decorate the page with sunflowers!

# I ♥ HATCHIMALS

These Hatchimal names have been split in half. See if you can put each one back together again! Choose a set of letters from group A, then match it up with the right set of letters in group B.

## GROUP A

ELE ~~ELE~~ DEER BUN HAM OWL PUPP

**HATCHY HINT:**

Struggling to see who's who? Look at each Hatchimal on the next page, then use the letter clues to work out the two parts of their name.

Write your answers here. The first name has been completed for you.

| A | B |
|---|---|
| ELE | FLY |
| | |
| | |
| | |
| | |
| | |

## GROUP B

ICORN IT STAR WEE ALOO ~~FLY~~

ELEFLY

PU_____T

_____NW

_____L_C___

D___R___O

H_M_____R

WELL DONE! GIVE YOURSELF A CUTE COLLEGGTIBLE EGG STICKER.

**DID YOU KNOW...?**

The best way to begin hatching your CollEGGtible is to rub the heart on the front to warm it up.

# STICK IT, QUICK!

This puzzle is a race against the clock! Set a watch or a timer to one or two minutes, depending on how fast you're feeling today. Then try to complete this rapid-fire quiz. Every answer is a sticker!

**1** Stick in a green Hatchimal.

**2** Stick in this Hatchimal's best friend, Kittycan.

**3** Stick in a Hatchimal who is full of springtime fun.

**4** Stick in an Elefly in a different color.

**5** Stick in a Hatchimal with tentacles.

**6** Stick in this Hatchimal's twin.

# JOIN THE PARTY!

Wow—it's a hatchy birthday party, and the whole gang is here! See if you can track down these three Hatchimals, who are hidden in the crowd. When you spot them, put a star sticker over each one.

**DID YOU KNOW . . . ?**

The rarest Hatchimal of all is Golden Lynx, from Moonlight Mountain!

# MAKE YOUR OWN HATCHY CARD

It's time to make your BFF smile! This hatchy card is easy to make and tons of fun. Cut out the template, then add your own cute sticker surprise.

## YOU WILL NEED:

♥ Scissors
♥ Colored pens or pencils
♥ Stickers from this book

HATCHIMALS™

## WHAT TO DO:

1. Cut carefully around the card template.

2. Write your message inside, color in the stars, then stick in a little Hatchimal.

3. Fold over the flaps one at a time. Tuck the last flap in, then seal it with the name label sticker.

4. Write the name of your BFF on the name label, and your card is ready to deliver to your special friend.

## SCISSORS ARE SHARP!

Check with a grown-up before you start.

# MY DREAM TWIN

Imagine if each of these cute little Hatchimals had a twin brother or sister! What would they look like? Use colored pens or pencils to color in each Hatchimal's imaginary twin.

Now decorate the page with sparkly heart stickers!

## DID YOU KNOW...?

Every Hatchimal is unique, and even a Hatchimal's twin doesn't look exactly the same as their sibling.

# GLITTERING GARDEN

It's time for a stroll around Glittering Garden! It's an enchanting place full of sparkling flowers and sweet scents. Take a peek into the blossoms and blooms. Can you spot the Hatchimals hiding in the picture?

Put a color sticker on top of each Hatchimal that you find.

Hatchimals come every day to the Daisy Schoolhouse for their lessons!

How many Hatchimals can you count?

DID YOU KNOW . . . ?

If you roll around in the sparkling flowers, you'll get covered in glitter from head to toe!

13

# TRAILS OF STARDUST

Can you help this little Deeriole? He has wandered off in Fabula Forest and lost the rest of his family. Follow the trails of stardust, then stick a magic toadstool next to the right route.

C

A B

FINISH

**DID YOU KNOW . . . ?**
Fabula Forest trees play music for Hatchimals that pass by!

14

# SQUAD GOALS

Look at these groups of happy hatchlings! Each frame contains friends from a hatchy squad, plus an extra Hatchimal who's hanging out with them for the day. Read the squad name, then draw a circle around the extra cutie in the group.

**1. BREEZY BEACH**

**2. RHYTHM RAINBOW**

**3. PETAL PATH**

**4. _____'S SQUAD**

NOW USE THE STICKERS YOU HAVE LEFT TO CREATE A BRAND-NEW SQUAD OF YOUR OWN!

# Answers

## PAGE 1

## PAGES 2-3
### HATCHTOPIA HANGOUTS!

## PAGE 4
### SURPRISE!

1. LIGULL    2. ZUFFIN    3. PUPPADEE

## PAGE 5
### FARM FUN

B E A D C

## PAGES 6-7
### I ♥ HATCHIMALS

| A | B |
|------|-------|
| ELE | FLY |
| BUN | WEE |
| DEER | ALOO |
| HAM | STAR |
| OWL | ICORN |
| PUPP | IT |

## PAGE 8
### STICK IT, QUICK!

1.     2.     3.

4.     5.     6.

## PAGE 9
### JOIN THE PARTY!

## PAGES 12-13
### GLITTERING GARDEN

There are 16 Hatchimals.

## PAGE 14
### TRAILS OF STARDUST
Stardust path B.

## PAGE 15
### SQUAD GOALS

1.

2.

3.

PAGE 10

WHO'S INSIDE?

IT'S A
SURPRISE!

TO:

FROM:

PAGES 2-3

PAGES 12-13

PAGE 7

PAGE 14

PAGE 11

PAGE 5

PAGE 9

PAGE 8

1.

2.

3.

4.

5.

6.

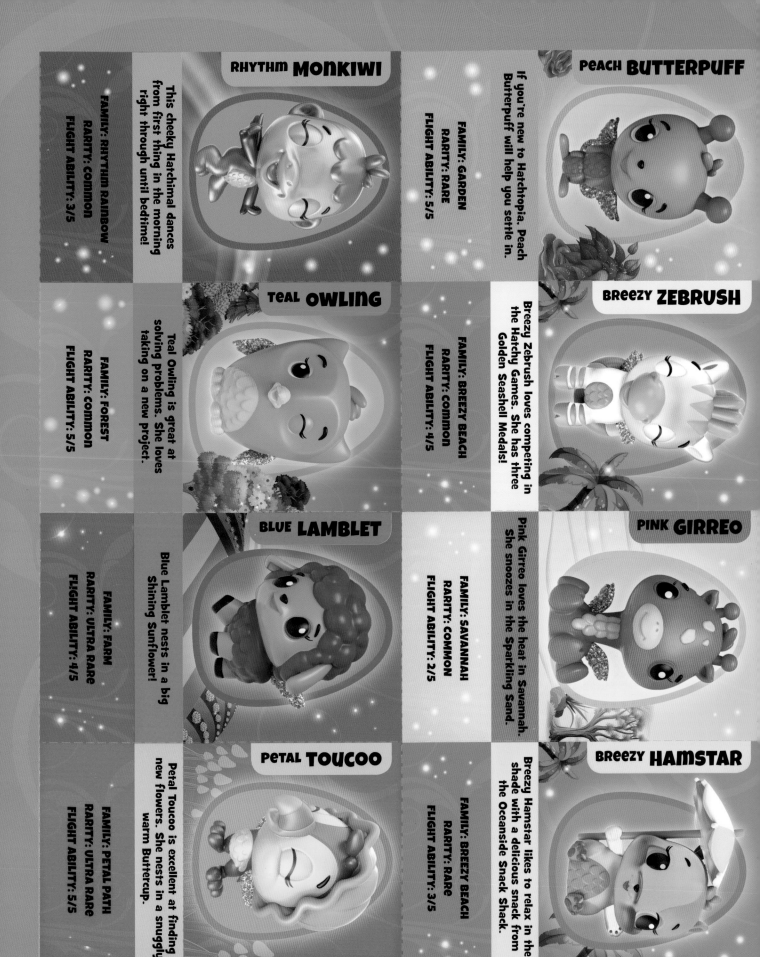

## PEACH BUTTERPUFF

If you're new to Hatchtopia, Peach Butterpuff will help you settle in.

FAMILY: GARDEN
RARITY: RARE
FLIGHT ABILITY: 5/5

## RHYTHM MONKIWI

This cheeky Harchimal dances from first thing in the morning right through until bedtime!

FAMILY: RHYTHM RAINBOW
RARITY: common
FLIGHT ABILITY: 3/5

## BREEZY ZEBRUSH

Breezy Zebrush loves competing in the Hatchy Games. She has three Golden Seashell Medals!

FAMILY: BREEZY BEACH
RARITY: common
FLIGHT ABILITY: 4/5

## TEAL OWLING

Teal Owling is great at solving problems. She loves taking on a new project.

FAMILY: FOREST
RARITY: common
FLIGHT ABILITY: 5/5

## PINK GIRREO

Pink Girreo loves the heat in Savannah. She snoozes in the Sparkling Sand.

FAMILY: SAVANNAH
RARITY: COMMON
FLIGHT ABILITY: 2/5

## BLUE LAMBLET

Blue Lamblet nests in a big Shining Sunflower!

FAMILY: FARM
RARITY: ULTRA RARE
FLIGHT ABILITY: 4/5

## BREEZY HAMSTAR

Breezy Hamstar likes to relax in the shade with a delicious snack from the Oceanside Snack Shack.

FAMILY: BREEZY BEACH
RARITY: RARE
FLIGHT ABILITY: 3/5

## PETAL TOUCOO

Petal Toucoo is excellent at finding new flowers. She nests in a snugly warm Buttercup.

FAMILY: PETAL PATH
RARITY: ULTRA RARE
FLIGHT ABILITY: 5/5